REACH YOUR HIGHER GROUND

PAULINE

Copyright © 2024

PAULINE

ISBN

All Rights Reserved. Any unauthorized reprint or use of this material is strictly prohibited. No part of this book may be reproduced or transmitted in any form or by any means, electronic or mechanical, including photocopying, recording, or by any information storage and retrieval system without express written permission from the author.

All reasonable attempts have been made to verify the accuracy of the information provided in this publication. Nevertheless, the author assumes no responsibility for any errors and/or omissions.

This is a True story.

Names have been changed to protect the innocent.

DEDICATION

This book is dedicated to my beautiful daughter Dee and all the mothers who struggle emotionally and financially and suffer from physical and mental abuse.

My heart goes out to all of you, as I know how this affects you, your children, and your life as it did ours.

I hope after all the pain you have endured, you find the peace, comfort, and true happiness you deserve.

PREFACE

We go through life searching for love, happiness, peace, and contentment. This is something we all want. But no matter what we wish for, most of the time, our life turns out to be the opposite of that.

Life can be complex, challenging, and difficult, but we are here to enjoy it despite these challenges. Difficult but not impossible.

I write this book for you all as an invitation to embrace the life you have. Do not let anyone or anything take away its joys, force you to live in despair and sadness, or make you feel unworthy. Take measures to change your life. Do not let anyone bury it, physically or mentally! Be happy. Life is too short.

Celebrate your life for all it can be for you and your children. The journey my daughter took shortened her life and left her children motherless. We all take paths in our lives, never knowing where they will lead us. Let yours be a "happy journey." If it's not the right path, take another.

Don't be afraid to take a chance. Embrace who you are.

TABLE OF CONTENTS

Chapter 1 1

Chapter 2 4

Chapter 3 7

Chapter 4 9

Chapter 5 12

Chapter 6 13

Chapter 7 17

Chapter 8 19

Chapter 9 21

Chapter 10 23

Chapter 11 24

Chapter 12 25

Chapter 13 29

Chapter 14 31

Chapter 15 32

Chapter 16 34

Chapter 17 36

CHAPTER 1

Dee, my daughter, to whom this book is dedicated, was the most adventurous and outgoing of all four of my children. Daring, to say the least. She wanted to do it all and stopped at nothing to do it.

She married young, 21. Although we always felt that she was not entirely happy, she stayed in the marriage for over 20 years.

She became a hairdresser and a very good one. While she loved it, it did not satisfy her thirst for music.

She took her guitar playing and singing to a new level and decided to go to Nashville. Her husband was all for it and encouraged her, thinking that she would be "discovered." She wrote a song, **"Reach Your Higher Ground,"** and recorded it, hoping it would someday take off. That song was among many, but her best one, **The Rain Said 'No.'**

Being her parents, we were against her leaving. She was leaving her family to embark on a career. A career that, unfortunately, would never happen.

However, she went to Nashville. It was her dream to sing at the Grand Old Opry. She sang at many clubs, including the **Blue Bird Cafe**, after talking them into listening to her. Thinking she would be discovered for her talent never panned out. There was more talent there than she expected, and she was never recognized. Her efforts were in vain, although she tried.

 She joined other singers, also wanting to be discovered. However, the competition was too great!

After a couple of years, she realized her dream would not ever be a reality. She was desponded and broke. Her marriage was not strong, and her husband, who was a Romeo, found the opportunity to play around and did so! Distance and time away were the final straw, and the marriage came to an end.

This led her to meet Don, who paid much attention to her, and she was flattered by the attention that he gave her. This she never had from her husband. Her husband played the field while she was away and had affairs. And, now, she was lonely and broke.

She thought she had finally met a man who would give her the love she was looking for and the attention she craved.

She had already decided that her singing and guitar career were not going anywhere, so she followed Don to TN, where he was from. She thought this would lead to a new life and happiness.

Their relationship continued. She really thought she had met a man who really cared about her. He was attentive and appeared to genuinely care for her.

During their relationship, she got pregnant and had a beautiful daughter. They appeared to be happy, but with time, she found that **he was not** the person he had put out to pretend to be. Another side of him began to emerge. A scary, mental person who was abusive. If nursing her daughter too long, he would come in and demand that she stop and go to bed. She was captive to all his sexual needs for hours at a time. She would also find him masturbating; anyone could walk into the room and find him in the act. It was frightening, she wrote in her journal.

However, she accepted his abnormal behavior and stayed with him. She was too ashamed to admit she made a huge mistake. She wanted to be a family, but her decision has turned out to be a horrible nightmare. A nightmare she was ashamed to share with anyone. **And afraid**. He was far from perfect, but the only thing that kept her bound to him was the fact that he was the father of her daughter. She thought he would change if they married, which he had promised.

He was so obsessive he would hide her clothes that he didn't want her to wear if he thought they looked too revealing or too tight.

Followed her to work to make sure that was where she was going. Not even a trip to the market would have been possible without her finding him there, too.

In reading her journal, I don't know how or why she settled for all this. She was such a strong woman. It pains me to even think about what she had been through without uttering a single word about it.

She had met her match, or so she thought, and he was wearing her down. This I could see with the events that took place in her life.

Yet, she never mentioned or shared any of this with her family.

Oh, I wish now that she would have. She should not have lived like this in fear and embarrassment.

CHAPTER 2

Unfortunately, they got married. They had planned a beautiful ceremony and had invited me as well. I had always been vocal about my displeasure with this marriage and her choice of life partner. So, when she invited us, I did not attend and told her that we were totally against this marriage and she was making a mistake. She didn't listen. She said he promised to take care of her and their daughter. She believed in him despite all the wrong he had done to her. And **she paid dearly later for this!**

Debrice, her sister, attended the wedding and had a long talk with Don, where he promised he would be a good father and husband.

She walked her sister down the aisle, hoping this marriage would be what was promised.

He was so "**odd**" and sick in many ways. She literally jumped from the frying pan to the fire with this marriage. She found out later that he never had any relationships prior to her. He found her to be interested in him, and she became his slave from then on.

His personality and attitude changed even more and got worse once they married. He went from Dr. Jekyll to Mr. Hyde. He was worse than she even thought.

While he was sweet as pie on one side, he became Satan on the other. Dee stays with him so they can bring up their daughter together, thinking he will change. He didn't. His sex drive was "obsessive" and sick. She was his sex object that he **abused for hours** and raped her numerous times every night. He would scream and yell if she didn't have sex with him and not let her go to sleep. This happened every night for years.

At times, she locked herself in the bathroom, but he would take the door apart to get in, she writes in her journal. He would punch himself in the face to make her feel sorry for him. He threatened to kill himself if he couldn't have her.

She was tired and trapped. She never knew what a sick, sick man this was that she had married.

My husband and I finally visited her after their marriage, wanting to meet who this guy was. We found out!!

Strange. The word is not strong enough to describe him. They picked us up at the airport in their beat-up car that had a temporary tire. My husband, feeling unsafe on the freeway, told him he would buy him a tire since there was a small child in the vehicle. My daughter had dropped to a level of living she was ashamed of and a husband even more ashamed of.

He answered back that he wanted "**four**" tires." Not even hesitating that we wanted more than what was offered without even knowing us. My husband, sensing his greediness, told him to forget the offer! **That was our first meeting**.

Just a few of the odd things that he said and did! He was dirty and unkempt. He appeared not to have showered for days. He smelled a foul odor.

We stayed a few days only to find out that, yes, he could be charming, but then turned a whole other direction when things did not go his way.

They had a beautiful daughter who we met and got to know. She was a darling. Seeing her, I wondered why Dee stayed. She **was afraid** to leave.

We were glad to finally leave but were **so saddened** to see what our daughter had gotten herself into and had to live with. As time went on, things only got worse.

 She visited us in California one summer with Don and their daughter, whom I will call Tara.

While there, he showed us his true "Don". He was not only domineering, he followed her everywhere to the point of stalking excessively. She could not be out of his sight for one minute. I questioned her later about his actions, and she admitted there was something mentally seriously wrong. It pained me to see her this way.

She wanted to leave him, but she was afraid he would not let her and take away Tara. Don had not worked for years and depended on his parents to provide for him, which they did! Even though he was perfectly able to work. He could not hold on to a job and never worked more than 9 or 10 months of the year. If that.

Well, he was in his forties, and they were still supporting him. They had no control over him when he went into his fits. Physical, yelling tantrums.

His mother doted on him and supported him in every way, no matter how wrong it was or he was. His family accepted and knew his behavior. My daughter always said his mother "wasn't all there," and when I met her, I was convinced she was right! Obviously, he was the chip off the old block! (mental)

Later, I will share what she wrote in her journal. It was difficult as a mother to read, in her own words, the life she was now living if it was a life!

We kept in close communication, and her sister would visit whenever she took off from work and on holidays.

We could see what was happening and told her that she had to leave. She knew, because of the clout his parents had, that he would take their daughter from her. It was a difficult time, and Dee was growing weary and frustrated with her situation.

Her hands were tied. She felt so trapped. Don had the upper hand and took advantage of it!

CHAPTER 3

Dee stayed married to him for several years. Afraid of him and what he would do if she tried to get away. My poor daughter had always been a strong girl and woman, and now we could see he was wearing her down. She was not the daughter we always knew. She was **"broken."**

She had gone from a strong woman to hopeless and powerless.

His obsession with her was getting worse. He would have fits, scream, and hit his head on the wall if he didn't get his way. He even threw himself in front of the car once, telling her to run him over. Telling her that he would kill himself without her.

Dee had been embarrassed and scared to tell us what was going on. We didn't know the full extent of horrors our daughter was living with that man until we saw it for ourselves when they came for a holiday, his actions were those of an insane person. His eyes even bulged, and it was difficult for him to keep control of his voice. He wanted to be everywhere she was and not leave her alone. I hugged my daughter when we were alone and asked her if she was OK. She shook her head, indicating, "No!" OMG, what had she gotten into? Who was this animal?

After she returned to TN, we started making plans for her to leave Don. This had gone way out of control, and it was not safe for my daughter to continue this way.

After a few weeks, she packed her few belongings and got some friends together to help her move into a small home several miles away while he was working, which was on a rare occasion.

He did not take to her leaving lightly. He haunted her at work and stalked her, and she had to have friends help her escape him. He found out where she had moved and harassed her constantly until the landlord who lived in front told him he would have the police arrest him if he returned.

He didn't come back to the house but was "always" around, **stalking, watching, and calling**.

For him to call fifty times in a row was insane. But he did. He was relentless. Day after day after day for months.

My daughter lived in fear, not knowing what he would do next.

He was capable of anything.

CHAPTER 4

Not too long after, I received a call from my daughter. The news she had was difficult to hear with all that she was going through. She was in tears.

She told me that she was pregnant. She thought it probably happened while in CA. It was overwhelming. Now, she had to go through this. Then she says, **it's twins**. We both cried. What should have been a very happy announcement was a very difficult time for my daughter.

She decided to have her babies. Abortion was not an option. And there were two.

It was a financial, emotional, and stressful time for her, to say the least. We cried and prayed that things would get better for her.

Her pregnancy was difficult, and we were not in TN to help through it. Being out of state was not easy for her or our family. She had no family there except for his. And, they, at this point, ignored her.

Of course, Don never mentioned that he would be of any assistance in any way, shape, or form to help with the babies that were coming. He totally denied that these babies were his and wanted no part of it. Nor did his family. She had gone into labor three times, and he nor his family ever came to help or see her.

Dee's older sister, Debrice, who was very close to her, was there for her as much as possible. They were always very close, even after Dee'ss marriage. It was difficult for her sister to see what Dee was going through.

My daughter Debrice knew from the beginning that Don was no good. She had warned her sister, but sadly to no avail.

Dee worked until her last day before her twins were born. She was huge, and we felt so bad with her in TN and us in CA. She would not leave TN because Don threatened to take Tara from her. She had a difficult childbirth. She had pneumonia, was overworked, alone, and broke.

She was depressed during the entire pregnancy and even suicidal with the situation as it was. It was more than she could endure at times. We kept in close touch with her, but we were all so far away. It was so difficult.

I was not able to get there on time for the delivery of her babies. However, Debrice was there, and I'm so glad that she was. She saw her nephew's birth. Paul and Gifford were beautiful, healthy babies. Identical twin boys were born in March of 2020. Her friends, knowing her situation, had a baby shower for her, and she received many items that were so needed.

When Don found out she had twins, he went to the hospital and created kayos. Screaming and yelling that he wanted to see the twins. Even though he had ignored her for nine months and denied he was the father**, there he was!**

He threw such a tantrum he had to be removed by security and restricted from the hospital. He was so out of control! She called me to tell me what had happened. She was so tired and sick. She had a difficult delivery. It was all she could do to get out of the hospital and home with the twins.

I went shortly after their birth. It was a difficult time for my daughter. I felt so helpless. She now had three small children to bring up and no husband to help **in any way.**

Postpartum was very difficult. She was so exhausted and **so depressed**. It was heartbreaking to see her this way. This was much more than postpartum, and we were concerned. With four children, I went through this, but never, never to this extent.

We stayed for a few weeks and then had to get back to CA as we had jobs waiting. It was such a sad time for us all. We hated to leave her and the babies and Tara to care for by herself.

When we left, we all cried and told her we would be there if she needed us. Just a phone call away. She had some friends who told her they would be there if she wanted them. It was Joyous and sad at the same time.

CHAPTER 5

These times were difficult for her. We wanted her to come to CA, but she knew Don would fight for Tara, and she could not leave her behind. So, she stayed in TN. He denied the twins and told all that they were not his. He referred to my daughter as a whore who had gotten pregnant with someone else's child. In this case, twins.

His mother referred to her new grandboys as the **"offspring"** and showed no emotion toward them whatsoever. Or even cared to see them. My feelings for her? I won't even mention it. She was the mother of hell, and Satan was her son!

We helped Dee start the divorce proceedings, knowing she could not continue living like this.

We helped her find an attorney to start the divorce process. Don was not happy with that and told her he would fight her till the end and would keep taking away Tara and that she would pay for this.

We found an attorney who appeared to be interested in helping with the divorce. She advised us that she knew of Don's family and the clout they had in the community. And warned us of this. Don's father was well-known and politically involved. And we were dealing with the southern **"good old boys"**! He knew many judges and entertained them at his home on occasion.

Don and his family made it "very clear" that this divorce would be a war!

What chance did my daughter have? They didn't take lightly to Californians and made that quite clear. They had clout and knew no one there who could or would help.

CHAPTER 6

Time passed, and now the twins were almost six months old and the cutest babies ever. The twins. So cute, chubby, and beautiful. My daughter was a great mom and loved her children dearly. We purchased a home for her in Woodstock so that she could have a decent home in a nice neighborhood for the kids. She appeared to be happy (for a short time).

Don's mother, who supported him in everything, would not admit that he was the father, which made me livid. They ignored the twins and never asked about them.

I despised her as much as I did, Don. What grandmother does that?

At the court proceedings, we all went. Dee, Debrice, and I. The twins were there; a friend took care of them while we were to be in the courthouse.

While we waited to go in, Don, his mother, and his attorney waited to also go in. Before entering the court, Don and his attorney approached us and presented a proposition that he would give her full custody of all the kids if he **did not have to pay any alimony**.

We looked at each other and thought, boy, **that would be great!**

We'd be rid of him once and for all!

Dee agreed, and we went into the courtroom. The attorneys each presented their case, and when it was presented that Don would not pay alimony and give full custody to Dee. The judge totally disagreed and advised that a father should be in their children's lives and that each should have custody. Since Don had a home with his parents, he could help with care and money. So, the judge decided Don would be in charge of this custody.

Since Dee could not work with twins and a small child, he thought it best to go with the father.

It didn't matter that these were babies, breastfed, and he had no job. The basis of the judge's decisions was only that he had a house and was with his parents!

When the kids moved to their house, they would tell Dee's daughter that her mommy didn't love her. On top of that, they would not let Dee speak to her when she called. Tara was always asleep and could not be awakened, they told her.

Concerning also was the fact that Don would masturbate with their daughter in the room they both slept in. In her journal, she also mentions that he sucks his thumb while this happened. Tara would also crawl all over him and touch his privates, and Don would not stop her or take her off of him. This was all so sick.

Tara began wetting and started biting herself. This coupled with the fact that when Tara came back home, she at one point started telling her mom that Grampa "poked" her with a pink stick in her privates and touched her. That's when Dee knew something was very wrong and that her daughter was telling her the truth. She knew too well that a child so young, only a five-year-old, does not makeup stories like this. My daughter reported this to the courts, and they sent Tara to the "Advocacy Center" for counseling.

They discounted the allegations and said it could not be proven. My daughter was heartbroken. Years of emotional and physical abuse, and now this! Her daughter, my granddaughter, was subjected to possibly a pedophile, and no one believed her. Why was Tara behaving like she was? She would speak of it out of the blue, and her description of what happened to her was in such detail that it was impossible to think that it was anything but truth.

Don's attorney said later it was another tactic from Dee to take the children away. Of course, he would say that. He was Don's attorney! Our family was sick, and Dee could not prove it. Only live through it!

This almost killed my daughter. We were so devasted and couldn't believe how any court, supposedly serving justice, could do this. They knew nothing about Don's background, or did they?

Also, Don was the one who presented the full custody issue. Don gave it one final blow, and he came back with the twins, saying they were not his, so he didn't want to have any obligation to them. The court ordered DNA and proceeded with the order to see if they indeed were his.

DNA'S came back, and of course, **they were his!** And while he wanted to play no part in their life, the court said "he" would have "full custody" of the twins! It was so unfair and unjust. I wish now that this judge knew of what a horrible, horrible, decision he made at that time. Again, Good Old Boy's state! We were from CA and didn't stand a chance!

It cost us all so much more than ever could be imagined.

Well, the court decision went on, and in the interim, our attorney, who was friends with the judge, dismissed herself from the case. In the middle of it all! We couldn't find another attorney that wanted to touch on this case!

It could not have been any worse. How do things like this happen? We had no leg to stand on, and everyone who was wrong was right!

We were able to find another attorney, and she knew the situation with the judge and the previous attorney. She advised that it would be difficult.

Several thousand dollars later, we were in no better shape than when we started, **but the divorce was finalized**, and Don still had the upper hand with the kids.

The court ordered each of them to get a psychological evaluation of both Don and Dee.

My daughter was evaluated as being "attentive and completely competent." She was also loving, caring, and responsive". Don, on the other hand, was found to be "negative and in lack of mutual support or care."

Yet, they deemed it suitable for Don to keep the custody and found absolutely no reason for Dee to have legal and full custody of the children. The situation with the kids stood as it was, and the kids suffered more than they had to with no mom to care for and love them as Dee could have with them being with her.

CHAPTER 7

Time did not heal any wounds for my daughter. Don was in his glory for "again" getting his way, and he took total advantage of it. The attorney we had was "useless" in trying to get the kids back, even in getting at least a half and half custody. It was now a fight not for justice but just to see them when it was rightfully Dee's turn.

They all went out of their way to make it unbearable and make Dee suffer. He changed the visiting days my daughter had with them, saying the kids were sick and could not be there. This happened more than we could count!

At times, he had "other plans" for them that day, etc. Anything to keep her away from her babies and daughter. His family would not let her speak to Tara and told her mommy didn't care about her or love her.

What a sick family to continue hurting not only my daughter but also Tara, a little helpless girl. My daughter became very depressed and cried a lot. We feared she contemplated suicide. He won! It was not because he was a good father or even wanted to be one. He was an evil person who wanted revenge. He was making her pay for leaving him just like he did in other ways when she was with him. Now that she finally wanted to get rid of him, this was payback time! He knew that he had lost her, and there was no way he could keep her bound to him, so he wanted to play his last dirty trick. Making her suffer for her children!

His mother, who was over seventy, took care of the "offspring," as she called them. They were always dirty, needed baths, and had dirty, wrinkled clothes when Dee picked them up. They never had socks to wear. Little Tara had long, matted hair. It was so obvious they were neglected while in their care.

This was all so heartbreaking. But the courts were "right" to keep them with their neglectful father while their loving mother's heart longed to even meet them occasionally. Wrong! No mother should have to go through this.

Dee always sent them back with haircuts, nails cut, clean clothes, new socks, and a fresh bath. And, with a **big hug and sad heart**. She was a "mom" and a great one at that!

Each time they left, it was a tearful event for her and the children. I prayed for my daughter and visited as much as we could. I prayed things would change. She shared these horrible events with us and her friends, who all knew how Don and his family were and what they were doing.

Life went on, sadly, never changing, and Don and his evil mother didn't care about the children at all. It showed in the way they looked, and they always came back hungry, dirty, and unkempt.

Don and his family were never going to change, and they made no bones about it. They loved that they had the upper hand. Their attitude was arrogant and defiant. Don and his mother would both go to pick up the children with smug looks. They knew they had won. I despised them for that.

They "gloated" in their victorious triumph. They conquered and overcame.

We were defeated! And so were the children.

CHAPTER 8

The years passed, and the children grew up. Dee took them every chance she could, even when he called to take them when he knew she had to work. That became a regular thing. Keeping a job in those conditions was not easy, but she wanted to be with her kids, even if it was for a short period.

She had to keep moving to different salons due to the schedule that Don had arranged. He knew she always had clients on weekends and was fully booked, but would call her to take them on her busiest days.

She took them anyway because she knew if not, he would not give them to her on her scheduled days. He didn't work, and he controlled the visiting days, which made it as difficult as he could.

She had clients who loved her and followed her wherever she went, and they all knew of Don's family and the situation. So, they were loyal to her.

God bless them!

Years passed with nothing changing. Don and his family continued to make life difficult for all. His actions were intolerable, and he displayed them often. The kids were growing up and accepted their lifestyle, but they were always so happy to come "home." Their own rooms, being fed and cleaned up, they were always in tears when they had to return to their father and grandmother, who was always smug when she attended to the pickup of the children.

With the passing of time, Dee made peace with the hell of a life Don and his family had created for her. Dee moved on, or more like tried to, "looking for love," but never really found it.

Don and his family continued as always, making it difficult for all. I really do not feel that they cared at all for the children. It was to pacify him and let him get his way. His actions were intolerable, and he displayed them to everyone. Nothing had changed.

Tara turned 13. I went to TN to celebrate her becoming a "teen." It was a fun time. Don and his mother were, unexpectedly, humane enough to let **me visit the kids** while I was there. They doted on the control they had. Evil is too kind for people like them!

They had not changed their tactics and threatened Dee each time she wanted to take the children on their birthdays or holidays. It was always **the day after** or not seeing them until the "**next**" scheduled time.

They punished her in any way they could. It was like this year after year. Nothing had changed and never would.

Christmas came around. The boys were now eight years old, Tara was a teen, and Dee was busy working at her job as a hairdresser. Her music nowadays came secondary, with everything else occupying most of her time. However, she played and sang at restaurants as often as she could. Playing the guitar, writing her own songs, and singing was her escape. She sang beautifully, and others seemed to enjoy her talents. Music was in her soul and got her through so many rough days. It was hope, a little something left in her life, that made her feel like herself, even if it was fleeting, and provided her little solace in the midst of the chaos her life had become.

CHAPTER 9

It was 2010, the holidays were here and a few days prior to Christmas I texted her and she wrote back that she had been busy at work and getting ready for the holidays and having the kids over. I was happy that she was happy and looking forward to seeing them. Baking and cooking all the things they loved. I heard back on Christmas Day from her, and she wished all the Ca family a happy holiday.

She was having friends over and doing a lot of cooking and baking for when the kids could come (**after Christmas**). Don never let her have them on holidays.

Two days after Christmas We received a call from her that she was waiting at the hospital to be admitted. She had a urinary infection, and she was having problems. She couldn't talk very much as she told me she was in a lot of pain and would call back later.

After I spoke to her, I felt very uneasy about her condition so I called her sister Debrice and told her that I would be leaving for TN. **Something was** very, very, **wrong,** I felt it!

She told me to also book her a flight and we would go together. Debrice wouldn't let me go alone and she now knows that would have been the biggest regret not to have gone. We both packed and left the next morning.

When we landed in TN I had a message that Dee's condition had worsened and we needed to get to the hospital ASAP!

When we arrived, getting out of the elevator we were greeted by Don and his mother who were asking us for **"forgiveness"**! Their guilt finally catching up on my daughter's deathbed. We hurriedly went past them and into ICU.

Upon entering we went to Dee's bed and when she heard our voices her eyes opened. We could see the fright in her eyes. I knew this was much more serious than we thought. She knew she was dying. We later heard that she called the priest for her last rites.

The nurse called me to the nurse's station where the doctor, Dr. Death, was on the phone to advise me **"your daughter's going to die"**. OMG what kind of a doctor tells a mother this, **on the phone,** with no emotion whatsoever. I think I died a little too. I 'll never forget that Doctor and the way she presented her message to me..

My daughter's' blood pressure was so low she had a stroke. The **doctor finally** came around and told us that if she lived, she would be an invalid.

It was the most devastating news a mother could ever hear. And she had three kids that so needed her. How could she die? Don and his family took away whatever time they could from her with the kids and now, it could be "forever".

She had many, many friends and clients come to visit wanting to see her and pray for her. She was so loved by all!

We never saw such a parade of support of friends. We all waited and prayed for better news. The nurses even asked me if she was a "celebrity".

if she was someone "famous" ? and I said **"yes"**! She is!!

The days following were the most difficult I ever had. My daughter was so ill, and the prognoses did not look good.

Her body was shutting down and it all looked so bleak. I felt I was living a nightmare and wanted to wake up. Why did all this happen? She did not deserve this.

CHAPTER 10

Don and his mother sat out in the waiting room to hear Dee's condition, as if they really cared. I didn't want him there or his mother. The Devils themselves, but I at the time was so distraught my only thoughts were of being with my daughter.

The days at the hospital were the most difficult for us. Debrice and I stayed and never left her side. Dee's blood pressure was so very low, and she was not responsive.

How could this be happening? She did not deserve this. And why, was Don and his mother out there when they never cared before. Guilt?

We all knew the situation was very serious. Tara would sit on her mom's bed and hugged her and told her to get well. I don't know if her mom heard her. Tears were in my eyes as she begged her mom to **"please get well"**.   Sadly, that never happened.

The boy's, too little to understand what was really going on were there with their father. They looked at their mom and told her they loved her. Never knowing they would never see her again.

CHAPTER 11

My daughter passed away on New Year's Day, 2011 a few days later. We all said our tearful goodbye. The children sat on her bed, hugged her. They didn't understand how final this all was and that they would never see their mother again. The twins were only 8 years old and Tara 13. Their mom was gone, forever.

She looked like an angel. So peaceful and beautiful. It was **so hard to let** her **go, knowing we would never see her again.**

This day would change the lives of her children to a life so devastating and heartbreaking no one could ever have imagined.

Don walked into the room and promised Debrice and I that he would take care of the kids and that we could call them and visit "anytime". He promised this to my daughter on his knees at her bedside with "fake" tears. Of course, that never happened. Hell is was too good enough for people like him.

We left the hospital with heavy hearts. A loss not knowing what or where to turn to.

What was to come, we never would have imagined. Losing a daughter, sister, friend and mother of young children was so difficult and sad but it would not end there.

When we returned to Dee's home, the laundry was still in the washer waiting to be dried. The Christmas tree was decorated with some gifts underneath waiting to be delivered.

All was so heartbreaking to digest. We never expected the holidays to end in such a sad, final way.

Don and his mother whisked the kids away and "promised" to let us see them, and to visit, and call them anytime we wanted. Don promised this with tears in his eyes. **It never happened**. And**, he had not changed.**

CHAPTER 12

A few months after Dee's passing, his parents couldn't tolerate three kids and Don now that my daughter was gone, there was no one to fight with for them.

He moved to Texas, where he could find work. Something he didn't do often. We went to visit the kids. They seemed happy. We took them shopping and to lunch and spent a few days with them. It was sad to leave them knowing they had no mom to be there to care and love them.

Don collected Social Security for all three kids. To him that was a lot of money, so he didn't work. Why would he if he could get by with it. All at the children's expense! This was now, his mode of living!

We stood a few days and went to various places with the kids we thought they would enjoy and bought things that were needed. We didn't see them again for a few years. Don moved from Texas and moved from state to state never letting us know where they were. His parents were of no help and advised me that they would let him know that we wanted to talk to the kids and send them things that were needed. This was all ignored.

We finally heard that he had moved to Virginia Beach. We went as soon as we could and visited with the kids. This time we were able to pick them up at their house. When I entered, it was such a **dirty, filthy mes**s. It looked like nothing was ever cleaned. Even the kids. It was heartbreaking.

We were advised that Gifford, one of the twins had been hit in the head and left almost blinded by his father when he taken the boys out surfing which they loved to do,

Don, in his stupor hit Gifford with the surfboard (unintentionally) causing him to almost lose his sight. Another one of his stupid episodes.

I cringed when I saw my grandson. This would never have happened in his mom's care.

Don was polite but anxious and didn't want us at the house. We left, picked up the kids later and took them shopping and to eat. We stayed for a few days. The boys played at the hotel pool and enjoyed themselves for once. They laughed and played, and it felt good to see them happy and laughing.

The few days spent with them were joyous for us all.

We said goodbye and asked them to call us if ever they needed anything.

I gave them postcards to send (postage paid) if ever they needed anything.

I truly believe Don took those away as we never heard from them.

It was always so sad to leave them never knowing what would happen next, where they would be or if we would be allowed to see them at all.

I made many calls to Don which he ignored. He never answered me. I made many, with no answer. I finally reached out to his father who was the "normal" one in the family. Or so I thought! He advised he would give Don the message. The **kids were always busy**, he said. Kids will be kids.

I waited and waited. Nothing! The only communication was with Don's father. I sent packages, money, food, but never heard back. Don moved from house to house because he didn't pay the rent and it was difficult to keep up with him. His father who was the only family member who communicated with me was "always vague". He gave me just enough information to satisfy me and told me he would have the kid's call.

Tara, when she turned 16 left and went back to TN to live with her grandparents. She was able to at least escape. We knew nothing of how the boys were. Only from Todd, the grandfather, that they were doing well and so was Tara who had moved with him and his wife, her grandmother.

If only she knew how these people had treated their mom..

But it was a chance of escape so we said nothing. Maybe in her later teen years she could have a normal life.

I spoke with Tara and she seemed happy to be with school friends again and would be there to graduate with them when it came time.

I was happy for her and told her so and that she had made the right decision.

I asked Todd when the boys should be graduating from middle school.

He told me that they were doing well and had above average grades. Nothing else. Again, to appease me. But I was happy to hear at least that.

Time passed again and no word from Don or how the kids were doing.

I texted Todd on a weekly basis knew I would get bits and pieces and no real answers. But better this than nothing from Todd!

He told me when I contacted him at one point that Don had covid and had been in the hospital for over a month. That it had been touch and go with him and one point was not sure if Don would make it. I guess I was supposed to feel bad about it. Instead, I asked, **where are the kids**? He advised, "with friends".

I later found out that he again had lost his rented house, and the twins were on their own. No food, or clothes. It was freezing cold, and they weren't going to school. How could "any" grandparent ignore this? He could have told me when we spoke but now, I feel he was trying again to protect his son so we would not know the conditions they allowed the kids to live in. We would have gone and taken the boys. Don unfortunately recovered from covid. No place to live, freezing cold, no job, so they all lived in his van, homeless. I later found out.

This was how he and his family took care of the children. Nothing had changed! How sad is this! All it would have taken was a simple phone call to us. We would have taken the kids in a heartbeat. Instead, it was his way. Again!!

To this date I cannot, cannot, understand how all that family allowed this and these poor boys to live like this. They were homeless and by themselves. They could not attend school, and didn't.

CHAPTER 13

The Paul and Gifford took after their mom and loved to play the guitar and to sing. They did this on the boardwalk in Virgina Beach to earn a few dollars for food I later found out. They were thirteen years old and playing for food.

Everyone liked listening to them. Two identical twin boys playing on the boardwalk and singing for whatever monies they could get.

With the few dollars they made they bought much needed items along with food that they didn't get much of. They loved performing. And people enjoyed listening to them. They were so proud.

They made enough money to purchase new guitars so their music would sound better. They hid a few dollars each time from their father who now had another means of making money. The kids playing guitar.

They got so good that the local restaurant hired them to play. This I was told by grampa Todd.

Tara went on to graduate from high school in TN. We went to see her at the ceremony. Don was there. Not at all receptive and avoided us as much as possible like the plague. We were able to see the boys for that day. We asked to pick them up the following day for breakfast and some shopping as we were sure they needed "stuff". When I called to tell them we were on the way to pick them up, we were advised by Todd, grampa, that Don had taken the kids and didn't know when they would be returning. We didn't see them again. Disappointed, we returned to CA. The same old, same old, excuses.

We heard later that they returned to VA Beach. To punish us is one thing. But to punish the kids over and over like that, I will never understand.

Don is mental, that I know for sure as well his mother. And his father went along with the program so as not to argue with them. So sad because innocent kids suffered dearly. No mom for them and a father who didn't care. Or the family that was supposed to be close and care for them., and didn't!

They kept all of us out of their lives for no good reason. Repeatedly they did this. They punished these poor kids for being born and gave them neglect and poverty. Only a sick family would do this.

The kids were not given a normal life and all kid's deserve one. And to keep us away as they did and poison their minds, tell them we didn't care or loved them is…unforgiveable.

Yes, the childen have all suffered emotionally, and physically because of this. They may or may not ever recover to a "normal" life. WE pray that they do. They so deserve it!

CHAPTER 14

On the boy's 18th birthday I decided, they are of age now, I can finally reach out to them. They can leave and do as they want without his consent. Don was in dire need now as he was not getting any more of my daughters' social security that he lived on for so many years so that he didn't have to work. Saving money for college or for their needs was out of the question.

I reached out and found that Tara was still in TN. She had not reached out to us since her graduation. I am sure they were told that we had disowned them and didn't care.

One of the twins had moved to HI. We found out on Facebook I asked Tod about that, and he advised me that Paul had left with a friend and Gabby was in MN with another friend. Both were doing well.

I was happy at least that they were no longer with their father and that they were "free". They did not try to contact any of us here in CA. I was not sure what was told to them or why they didn't. We were always here for them and we told them all that.

I sent a card to Paul where I thought he was living and to my surprise, I got a response. He seemed happy to hear from me and I was overjoyed. He told me he was in Maui and was very happy living there. He sent photos of himself. What a handsome young man. He told me he spoke to his brother often, but he had gone back to his father. I was so disappointed to hear that.

CHAPTER 15

We decided that we, Debrice my husband and I would go to Maui and visit with Paul now that he had reached out. We were all so excited. This was in November before Thanksgiving. We spent a week with him. What a wonderful young man he had grown to be. He seemed to be happy, playing the guitar and singing. Just like his mom liked to do.

He shared with us that he had no recollection of his mother and barely remembered her. He was only eight when she passed. His father never showed them photos or spoke to them about her, he said. Nor her family, us, as if we did not exist.

In our visit, he advised us that when his father got covid, they had no place to live. They were evicted from the house they rented. Once Don was released from the hospital, stayed at the Residence Inn for a few days. While there he met a nice lady next door who had invited the boys over for dinner because "they looked hungry". She befriended them and fed them while she was there. She was on a job assignment for a short while. While there Pat got ill and had a hernia that almost burst. The nice lady next door had not seen him for a few days and asked his brother about him. When she heard he was ill, she took it upon herself to go check next door and found Paul doubled over in pain. She told Don who was perturbed about her coming over, to get him to a doctor ASAP. He told her that his son would be alright.

Being in the hospital business she knew something was wrong and that he needed attention right away. She took him personally the next day to the hospital. It turned out he had a double hernia and needed surgery immediately.

Had she not taken him, he would not be here today. Bless her heart for this.

Paul had his surgery and was getting ready to be released when the nice lady advised him that she was transferring to Maui and would be leaving in the next day or so. Paul told her if he went back to the hotel, his father would not care for him and he would probably die from lack of care and filth that was in the apartment. Mia, the nice lady invited him to come along and get a new life with her in Maui.

Since he was now 18, Mia, the nice lady, told him he was now of age and could go and do whatever he pleased. He told her he would go with her. He had no license, birth certificate or passport. But they pulled this off and he went!

CHAPTER 16

It was the best thing that could have ever happened. What a wonderful opportunity. Don was furious but there was nothing he could do. Paul was now 18 and could finally get out of his father's clutches and leave behind that deplorable life he had been subjected to live.

It is now three years later; he is a very happy young man and Mia is happy to have him with her. The son she never had.

We met her while on our visit to Maui. She introduced herself and told us how she met Paul and the story he told her of how he lived.

She has given him a new life and he has come back into ours.

It saddens all of us that my daughter's children, our grandchildren, had to endure this life with a mentally ill, sick person. His parents knew the situation. But it was always, they are fine, kids are always too busy to call, etc. Of course, we knew Don would never contact us. He was probably afraid we would take the kids away. Even when they so desperately needed our help. We never knew. How sad is this.

Today. Paul is doing well. Is continuing school, that he never finished, his brother, Gifford unfortunately, has gotten into drugs and is having mental issues as well. He is trying to get help. We pray for him. His father has a hold on him and he is so vulnerable.

Tara is working in TN and is doing Ok for now. We keep in touch and are here if she needs us. She is 25 years old. She grew up in her teens without a mom and I know that was so tough for her. She knows her father's mental state and keeps away. I am not sure if she remembers her grandfather and what he did, or what she said he did. I am afraid to ask.

Best not to if she does not remember.

Paul disowned Don and says he is not his father and wants no part of him. He refers to him only as Don.

I am not sure if Don tried anything sexual with the kid's. My feeling is, YES!

They lived aa a terrible life and that family made sure we did not contact them to protect their mentally deranged son. The kid's they proved to us all, they didn't care what happened to them.

Had my daughter lived this would never have happened. These kids would have had a "normal" life. Happy and with a loving mom.

In turn, they had Don and the judge who gave him full custody of three kids to a mentally sick, sick man and deranged family.

CHAPTER 17

Paul now plays guitar and sings and wants to do this professionally. We'll see. But for now, all we want is that these young kids to have a decent life and can now move forward.

As I close this chapter, Gifford, his twin brother is now working and working on himself to get a better life. We are so happy to hear life is turning around for him as well.

It has been a life in despair and now we are in hopes that they can live a full life, get the help that they also need to overcome the tragic lives they have lived. They had a huge injustice given to them and the courts were so wrong in their decisions.

The children, now grown, can now reach out to all of us. And they have. We are here, they know this, and know that they are loved and we will support them and want them to be as happy as they deserve to be.

In closing, I just want to reach out to all you moms who are going through this. I know there are many of you. The courts are not always right, and our kids are then put in the wrong hands as ours were.

There was no justice for them, and we lost not only a daughter, but our grandchildren as well.

Today, Don looks shabby, dirty and lives in a van. Jobs he gets, whenever he can. He is destitute. But he appears to like that lifestyle. We are just so grateful the kid's don't have to.

He calls them all on a very regular basis trying to get them back.

To return to live with him. Hopefully, they don't. He is their father and they do not know anything else. He never even shared photos of their mother or spoke of her so the boys who were so young do not remember their mom except for her keys when she placed them on the counter and her "delicious spaghetti". Funny, kids will remember mom's cooking.

I pray for you all. **Be strong**, stay strong, and seek help! Let someone know, share your feelings! Don't let this happen to you or your children! **Leave** don't stay. My daughter thought it best to stay and see what it did to her and the children. We not only lost a daughter but three grandchildren as well.

She reached her higher ground but not as it was intended.

With love and prayers all to you.

This story will continue with prayers for a positive outcome for all.

www.ingramcontent.com/pod-product-compliance
Lightning Source LLC
LaVergne TN
LVHW061049070526
838201LV00074B/5235